Aliens and Androids

A Quirky Collection of Funny and Touching Science Fiction Short Stories

J.J. Harlan

Copyright © 2019 J.J. Harlan

All rights reserved.

ISBN: 9781091487208

DEDICATION

To My Dad:
For filling my head with dreams of outer space, UFOs, talking animals, creatures from distant worlds, and other such wonderful, magical nonsense. I'm eternally grateful.

Sign up for our mailing list and be entered to win a FREE autographed copy of any of J.J. Harlan's books. New winner selected every month!

Sign up here:

https://mailchi.mp/f934c2e6967c/jjharlan

CONTENTS

	Acknowledgments	i
1	A Likely Excuse	1
2	Electric Raspberries	Pg 4
3	World War None	Pg 19
4	Safari	Pg 22
5	Patent Pending	Pg 33
6	The Countdown of a Lifetime	Pg 38

ACKNOWLEDGMENTS

I owe a tremendous debt to my wife for her feedback, ideas, and encouragement. Thank you for all the help, as well as the years of patiently listening to my far-fetched story ideas.

A LIKELY EXCUSE

"Not again, not again, not again," Orril Bax chanted. He knew his chances of making it to the clan gathering on time were slim. The unexpected asteroid field had caused a huge delay, and he was angry with himself for not updating the navigational charts before departing. He needed speed, he needed luck, and he needed them now. Orril gritted his fangs and wiped a trembling paw across his cold, wet nose.

The particle engines on his sleek rocket roared as he streaked through the dark voids of space. Orril knew his cruiser was fast but was it fast enough? Despite his pressing need for speed, he remained wary. There were too many stories of unsuspecting travelers and their encounters with Grogans in these distant parts of the star system.

Still, he would brave anything in order not to be late, again, to the gathering. The first time was awful, but a second time... The very thought of angry clan elders made his tail twitch. He pictured them sitting behind their benches, their brows deeply furrowed as they debated his punishment. He could already hear their furious shouts of righteous indignation. With shaking, gnarled claws they would point at him and pronounce judgement for his transgression. Orril gulped.

Pushing the throttle forward, he felt the hull of his craft rumble, the thrusters thundering with maximum power. He veered into the interplanetary cargo zone, a slow shipping sector off-limits to tiny cruisers like his. Sure, it was dangerous, but it might save precious time.

He adjusted his course and zigzagged between the glowing space buoys. An electric thrill flooded Orril's body as power beams from the buoys grabbed his tiny ship and flung it headlong through the flight corridor. He double-checked his scanners. He wanted no other unexpected "surprises" out here, and he certainly did not want to run into... *them*.

While approaching the moons of Durlune, Orril glanced at his chronometer and cursed. It took all of his mental strength to suppress the horrifying thoughts of what punishments might await him if he was late. Orril squeezed the control yoke and pleaded in vain with the unsympathetic, inanimate rocket. "Faster, for the love of all that is sacred, faster—"

He zipped between the moons, excited thinking about pulling off the impossible. Suddenly, the ship's proximity sensors blinked a warning. A shrill alarm sounded in the cockpit; Orril instinctively pulled back the throttle and checked his instrumentation panel. He glanced at the flashing monitors and confirmed his fears—Grogans.

They must've been lying in wait behind a moon when they'd spotted him. For a moment, Orril contemplated escape. If he could just get to Durlune's atmosphere, he might be able to... no, he couldn't chance it. They had far superior ships, and if he tried to run, it would all be over. The best decision, the *only* decision, would be to capitulate—to let them board. A cold, sick feeling of dread churned in his gut, and he grudgingly accepted the Grogan flight command codes. With a stroke of a key and the flip of a switch, both ships fell into a complementary flight path.

The Grogan vessel pulled alongside the little cruiser and extended a boarding portal. A loud metallic clang echoed in Orril's ears as the portal docked with the cruiser's airlock, and a hiss of compressed gases clarified it: the two ships were now connected. Orril's dual hearts raced in syncopated fear as he stood and nervously stepped to the door.

The cruiser's metal hatch swung open, and through it strode a monstrous figure wearing a blue uniform. The Grogan sniffed the air with his large snout and grimaced. Saliva glistened on a pair of hideous tusks jutting from the corners of his mouth. The Grogan adjusted his mirrored flight glasses and hitched up the weapons belt at his waist. He glared down at Orril's tiny, trembling frame. With military precision, the creature whipped a holopad out of his breast pocket and flipped it open.

"Sir," the Grogan growled, "do you have any idea how fast you were going back there?"

ELECTRIC RASPBERRIES

Aside from the fact that she was slowly dying, Martha was feeling rather upbeat about her day. Sure, she was tired from the bouts of vomiting last night, but a generous dose of morphine had dulled her pain. The nausea was receding and, for now, she was somewhat comfortable. *Hell*, she thought, *I suppose any day not spent writhing in agony is a good day.*

After pouring herself a cup of mint tea, she debated how she might spend the next few hours of respite. Her thoughts were interrupted when a chime alerted her to a visitor at the front door. She grimaced, her hopeful attitude evaporating thinking about having to expend her limited energy this morning, but it had been weeks since her last visitor and she was lonely. She tied her robe and shuffled down the narrow hallway, steadying herself with a hand against the wall as she went. The doorbell chimed again.

"Yes, yes, I heard you the first time," she muttered. Opening the door a crack, she peered out.

"Who are you?"

A man in clean, pressed medical scrubs stood on her doorstep. He wore a blank expression and a nametag. A large travel bag was slung over his shoulder. His bright blue eyes matched the color of his uniform.

"Hello, Martha Patterson," he said. He pointed to his nametag, "I am TL-66, your Personal Care Unit."

She stared at him for a long moment. "Well, that was quick. My doctor just referred me to your services yesterday." She squinted her eyes to get a better look. "Hmmm... They weren't kidding, you sure do *look* human. Come in." She opened the door and motioned for him to enter.

Martha eyed her guest with uncertainty. "So," she said after shutting the door, "you're a robot, eh?"

"Not quite. Technically, I am an android."

"Are you human?" she countered.

"No."

"If I sliced you open would I see bits of wire and sheets of metal and plastic?"

"Yes."

"Do you run on batteries or something?"

"Yes."

"Then, *technically*, you're a robot, plain and simple." She crossed her arms and slowly circled him, taking in his athletic build and neatly trimmed blond hair. She stroked her chin in guarded amazement. "But my, oh my, they do make you look human," she repeated.

"I'm sorry, is there something wrong? Older models are available if you wish—"

"No," Martha interrupted. "You're fine. This is just... a strange situation. I don't know why my doctor thinks that if the nurses can't take care of me properly, a robot would somehow do the trick. Still… you're someone to talk to. It's a good thing my insurance is paying for this ohhh—" Martha felt herself swaying and leaned against the wall to catch her balance.

The android flung out his arm to steady her. "Are you all right?" he asked.

"Yes," she said, "it's… it's the pain meds. They make me feel dizzy sometimes."

He stepped towards her. "Would you like to sit down?"

"Sure, help me to the couch." She grabbed his arm, surprised at how strong and solid he felt. He helped her to the living room where she eased herself onto the cushioned sofa. "That's better," she sighed.

"Can I get you anything?" he asked.

"Would you please bring me my tea from the kitchen?"

He hurried away but quickly reappeared with the steaming drink. He handed it to her then stood at attention as if waiting expectantly for a new request.

"Thank you," she said, sipping her tea. "Will you please sit down?" She squirmed in her seat. "You're making me nervous hovering over me like that."

The android scooted a chair closer to the sofa, laid down his bag, and sat. Martha thought he looked almost military in his posture, arched back with hands on his knees.

"Well, what should I call you?" she asked.

"I am TL-66," he said, "although I have been programmed to respond to any name of your choosing."

"Hmmm…" she said, "I've always been partial to 'Jack.' May I call you 'Jack'?"

"As you wish," he replied.

"It's a good name," she smiled a little. "How many times have you done this, Jack?"

Jack tilted his head. "Done this?"

"You know, help someone who's… dying? How many patients have you had in the past?"

"I am a new model, you are my first patient."

Martha sat her tea down on a side table and leaned back into the cushion. "You mean to tell me, you've never done this before?"

"I am programmed with all necessary medical and nursing skills," he elaborated. "In addition, my system performance and patient satisfaction rates will improve in time. The more experience I gain, the better I will become at serving my patients."

Martha pursed her lips and shook her head. "My doctor told me you wouldn't be like one of those clunky hospital room robots, and all this fancy technology may make you look like a 'real' nurse, but you're just a walking, talking computer, aren't you?"

Jack blinked. "The more human interaction I have…" he paused as if calculating his next words, "the more human-like qualities I will manifest in time."

Martha rolled her eyes. "In the meantime, I get to deal with the rookie. Alright, what is it that you'll do, exactly?"

At this question, Jack's rigid posture softened, and he leaned forward in his chair.

"I am here to help you," he explained. "I am here to assist with daily activities, medication administration, and to provide companionship and comfort."

"Comfort?" Martha snorted. "From a robot?"

Jack was about to speak, but Martha cut him off, "I know, I know—you're not a robot." She picked up her tea again.

"Okay," she raised an eyebrow. "What do you know about me?"

"I know your name, age, address, and medical history," he recited. "I am also aware that you were not satisfied with your two previous care providers."

Martha dismissed his comment with a wave. "See here, to those other nurses I fired, I'm just a paycheck. They don't know what it's like to be a lonely woman at the end of her life. I couldn't stand all that phony sympathy, it made me even more nauseous than I usually am. Besides, at the time I didn't need that much help." She took a sip of tea and motioned for him to continue.

"In addition, I am thoroughly knowledgeable concerning your medical diagnosis: pancreatic cancer."

Martha frowned. "Please don't say that word around me. I'm sick of hearing that word."

"Which word?" he asked.

"The 'C' word."

His voice lowered in volume, "I shall not say that word again."

"Thank you."

"You are welcome, Martha," he replied.

Jack looked thoughtful for a moment. Martha imagined tiny sprockets and gears whirring away in his head.

"Martha, it appears I am lacking some medical information, what is your estimated life expectancy?"

She frowned again, "My, you're blunt, aren't you? What, are you already eager to leave?" She avoided his gaze and picked at the fraying edge of her robe. "The all-knowing doctors told me I had twelve weeks to live."

"When did they say that?" he asked.

"About twelve weeks ago. To be honest, I've been avoiding hospice."

"Oh," Jack said. "Why did you wait so long to ask for assistance?"

Martha winced. Now it was her turn to reflect, "Because asking for help meant admitting I was going to die. I guess I was just scared." She inhaled deeply. "Hell, I *know* I'm scared." She pulled a loose string from her sleeve and let it fall to the floor. "My family and my friends, they're are all gone now, and nobody wants to die alone."

"Oh," Jack said again.

***

The following morning, Martha poked a spoon at the bowl of bland oatmeal in front of her. It was one of the few things she could eat without feeling queasy, but she was tired of tasteless, monotonous dishes. She missed the savory cuisines that once tickled her palate. Her food now was a lot like her life, flavorless.

She put down the spoon and let her eyes wander to a faded photograph, lovingly framed and hanging on the wall. A smiling man holding a laughing little girl stared back at her. So many memories from so many years ago flitted through her mind and she closed her eyes to enjoy them.

The ringing of the phone broke her from her thoughts. It was Dr. Benton calling to check on her. He asked if the new medications were helping with the nausea and he wanted to know how she was getting along with her Personal Care Unit.

"He's okay, I suppose," she said, "but I still find the whole idea bizarre. I guess…" she paused, "I guess he's better than the others."

"You know, we discussed other options," Dr. Benton reminded her, "and you've discharged all your human nurses. Would you reconsider a hospice facility—"

"No," she interrupted. "I'm staying at home. I'm not going to die in some godforsaken nursing home where patients are packed in like sardines. Besides, Jack seems to be a help—"

"Who's Jack?" Dr. Benton asked.

"He's the robot, sorry, I mean 'android.'"

"You named him?"

"Yes, I did. I'm not calling out a jumble of letters and numbers every time I need something."

Dr. Benton went quiet for a moment. "That's fine, Martha. I'm glad he's doing the job, I suppose." He cleared his throat. "Please let me know if we need to make adjustments in your medications, or if you change your mind about checking into a facility."

Martha promised Dr. Benton she would let him know, and, yes, the new medications were helping with the nausea. She didn't mention the fact her discomfort was constant now, or that her prescribed morphine dosage just wasn't cutting it anymore.

She hung up the phone and called for Jack.

He quickly appeared at her doorway. "Hello Martha, how may I assist you?"

"Can you please make me a hot bath?"

"Of course, Martha. I would be happy to do that for you."

Martha watched as he disappeared into the bathroom. Like a faithful dog nuzzling its master, Jack's eagerness to please was apparent. Throughout the night he had acted as though his very existence depended upon helping her. She supposed, in a way, it did.

"For future reference, Jack, baths help with the pain."

Jack popped his head around the door.

"You know, it might help other patients... later on," she explained.

"Yes, perhaps it will, Martha."

Mostly to herself, she continued, "My Daddy always said, 'Baths are not only good for the outside of the body, but for the inside as well.'"

While he filled the tub, she slipped out of her robe. She tried to recall the last time she wore 'real' clothes. The last time she wore anything other than bathrobes or pajamas. It seemed like a lifetime ago. It *was* a lifetime ago. Whatever it was she had now wasn't her life. It was just one prolonged, painful interlude, a commercial to be waited through before the end of the show.

Lazy wisps of steam followed Jack as he reemerged from the bathroom. "May I assist you into the bath?" he asked.

"If you would, thank you," Martha said. She put her arm around him and they both made their way cautiously to the tub.

"I'm not much for modesty anymore," she chuckled. "I guess after enough doctors and nurses see you naked, and not to mention those drafty hospital gowns, you lose your sense of propriety."

He gently lowered her into the warm water and

she slid down the porcelain.

"Ahh, that feels lovely," she sighed and closed her eyes.

"I am glad," Jack said. He sat down on the edge of the tub. "Is it alright if I stay in here with you?"

She opened her eyes, "Why? Are you worried I'm going to drown?"

Jack smiled but said nothing.

"Oh, you *can* smile, can you? That's much better than your 'serious face.'" She tried her best to imitate Jack's usual expression. "Keep it up, you might just become a real person," she said with a wink.

His smile widened.

A thought crossed Martha's mind, and she bit her lip and smirked.

"Please don't take this the wrong way, but I'm morbidly curious…"

"Yes, Martha?"

"Are you like a human in *every* way?"

"In every way?" Jack questioned.

"You know… Do you have all the *man* parts?"

Jack appeared momentarily confused but then nodded his head. "Are you referring to sexual genitalia?"

Martha tittered. "Yes, I'm referring to that."

"I am programmed and enabled to provide all manners of physical comfort, including sexual relations," he replied. "Do you wish to have sexual relations, Martha?"

Martha threw her head back and laughed. "No, thank you, Jack," she grinned, "but thanks for the offer. I haven't been immorally propositioned in a long time!"

Jack smiled at her again, "You are welcome,

Martha."

***

A few nights later, Martha bolted upright in bed, her hands clutching the sheets in balled fists.

The excruciating pain was back.

The first punishing wave ripped through her body and sucked the breath from Martha's lungs. She curled into a fetal position and screamed for Jack. Within seconds he was at her bedside.

Martha could barely utter the words as she rocked back and forth on her side, "Help, it hurts." She pulled her knees to her chest and clenched her teeth; the torment so relentless she couldn't even manage tears. Lightning was in her bones and at any moment she might explode.

Without a word, Jack went to task. He whipped open a medicine pack on the nightstand and drew up a syringe full of Dilaudid. He plunged it into her vein at a measured speed and then drew up another dose to have at the ready. He prepared a different medication to counter nausea and injected her again.

Martha felt the sting of the needle followed by a cool sensation washing over her body. The glorious narcotic was taking effect. Gradually, the stabbing agony became more bearable, and she realized she was holding her breath. She took in a shallow gulp of air and exhaled.

"Thank you, Jack. I think the pain is subsiding a little."

"You are welcome, Martha." His voice was soft.

"I'm sweating," Martha said. "My head feels like it's on fire."

With a delicate touch, he brushed the hair from

her damp forehead. "I can adjust my skin temperature," he said, "Would you like me to cool you?"

"Yes, please."

He held his palm to her forehead, and a refreshing coolness caressed her skin. He placed his other hand under the back of her neck and soothed her with his touch.

"That's so nice," Martha said. She managed a weak smile. "Neat trick."

***

The next morning brought with it bright sunshine and a lilting melody from a sparrow outside Martha's window. Its song floated on the breeze and roused Martha from her sleep.

She opened her eyes to see Jack sitting on the side of her bed, his hand resting on hers. She yawned. "How long have you been there?"

"All night," he said. "I never left you. I hope that does not make you feel nervous?"

"No," she said, "it's nice and I'm glad for it." She propped herself up in bed and took his hand in her own. "Mmm… Now it feels nice and warm." She held his hand to her cheek.

"How are you feeling?" he asked.

"Right now?" she said. "I'm not in too much pain, but I feel so drained."

"I mean about… dying."

"Oh," she said.

"Are you still feeling scared?" he asked.

"Always," she nodded, "It's a lingering fear that never goes away. It wraps itself around every thought and even creeps into my dreams."

"I am sorry," he said, lowering his eyes. "I enjoy helping you, and I do not like to see you scared."

Martha smirked, "Why Jack, are you feeling sad? My, my, they really *do* make you as human as possible, don't they?" She touched his cheek and wondered aloud, "Do androids ever feel afraid?"

"The thought of your death," he said, "makes me feel as though... something has malfunctioned within me, or as if I am low on power." He folded his hands in his lap. "I do not want you to die, and to me, this is 'fear.'"

She looked deeply into his delicate blue eyes and noticed for the first time how truly lifelike they were.

"Maybe it's just your programming?" she offered.

"Perhaps," Jack stared at his hands, "but that does not make it feel any less real to me."

Martha was reminded of someone gentle and kind from many years ago. She swallowed the lump in her throat. Was it possible a machine could do this?

"You know what I'm not feeling anymore?" she said.

Jack looked up but didn't reply.

"Alone," she said. She squeezed his arm, "And I'm glad to know someone will miss me," she added.

Martha turned her head towards her window. The August sun poured the last of summer's golden rays through the cracks in the blinds. "Could you please let the light in, Jack?"

He rose from the bed, went to the window, and pulled the blinds wide open. Sunlight flooded the room and Martha closed her eyes. She felt the warmth on her face and beamed.

"Do you know what I'm thinking about right now,

Jack?" she said, her eyes still shut.

"What, Martha?"

"Raspberries."

"I will get you some if you like," he replied. "Do you have any in the kitchen, or should I place an order with the grocer?"

"Not that kind, Jack. The ones my daddy used to give me. I'm afraid you can't buy those in a store."

A puzzled look spread across Jack's face. "I do not understand. Were they berries?"

Martha smiled and patted the bed. Jack walked over and sat next to her.

"On bright summer days like this one, when I was a little girl, my daddy and I would play in the fields behind our house. I would run and he would chase me and catch me and twirl me around in the air. I would giggle, and he would bury his face into my tummy and blow until I laughed so hard I couldn't breathe. Then, we would do it all over again. My daddy called them 'raspberries'."

Martha stared at the sunshine streaming through the window and sighed. They both sat in tranquil silence.

In one confusing moment, Jack reached out and patted her on the head. He slid closer to Martha and gently lifted her shirt. She grinned when she realized his intent. He slowly lowered his head to her stomach, his lips tickling her skin. With an awkward motion, Jack tried blowing a raspberry. The clumsy attempt made Martha giggle. She laughed even harder when Jack tried again. By the third try, Martha was laughing so hard tears rolled down her cheeks.

A bewildered Jack raised his head, "Is this what you wanted?" He bent over again and blew even more vigorously.

Martha slapped her hand on the bed in mock submission. "I give up, I give up," she squeaked out. "No more, I can't—"

He stopped blowing and Martha caught her breath in slowing gasps.

She wiped her eyes and basked in the lingering euphoric glow. "Thank you, Jack."

"You are welcome, Martha. Were those suitable raspberries?"

"They were wonderful."

***

That night, Martha shivered in her bed. She pulled her thick blankets close and curled into a ball. "Jack, I feel so cold. Can you please lie with me and warm your skin?"

"Yes, Martha, I will."

Maybe it was just her imagination, but lately, it seemed the mechanical rhythm of his speech had smoothed itself into a gentle and calming voice.

Jack climbed into bed and slipped under the covers. Wrapping his arms around her, he pulled her close.

Martha sighed, drinking in the warmth and compassion emanating from his synthetic skin, and for the first time in a long while, she felt no pain. She was tired– very tired – but the pain was completely gone.

"Jack?" she said.

"Yes, Martha."

"I'm not scared anymore. I don't know exactly why, but I feel… safe now. Like I did when I was a little girl."

Jack pulled her closer. "I'm glad for that, Martha."

Her eyelids grew heavy and she nuzzled his chest. After a long, quiet moment she spoke, "Do you know what my daddy's name was?"

Jack lifted his head. "No," he said. "What?"

"It was 'Jack.'"

Minutes ticked by before he broke the silence.

He shifted slightly and whispered in her ear, "Martha?"

"Yes, Jack?"

"Thank you."

"No, thank *you*." she murmured, then closed her eyes to dream of summer.

WORLD WAR NONE

The aliens landed on the lawn of the United Nations building on a sunny Thursday afternoon. Somehow, their silvery craft had slipped past U.S. radar and air defenses and gently hovered down to the soft, summer grass.

Within five minutes, groups of pedestrians gathered to ogle the unusual spectacle. Within thirty minutes of the landing, police, firemen, medics, photographers, news crews, and men in masks wearing bright yellow hazmat suits joined the growing congregation. Within the hour, the president and politicians, along with their advisors and the advisors' advisors, deliberated and debated about the topic of "What the hell are we going to do about the alien invasion?".

It was the almost universal consensus of the top U.S. military brass to "immediately nuke the bastards back to the galaxy from whence they came." However, others in the government suggested this would be a significantly unpopular decision among the New Yorkers residing in the area around the United Nations. So, grudgingly, the idea was vetoed.

It was General Blackwell who then suggested they build a large, secure wall around the craft to protect the populace (and, of course, prevent foreign prying eyes from lusting after the gleaming interstellar technology). This plan seemed much more acceptable, and the gathered politicians clapped the general on the back, and shook hands, and were proud they had made a wise decision that probably wouldn't upset their constituents.

However, before congratulations were finished, the plan had to be put on hold for the door to the craft unceremoniously slid open.

A plank lowered from the belly of the craft to the ground. Screams and gasps of surprise rippled through the crowd as two of the vehicle's occupants stepped out onto the plank. Their stretched, gangly bodies shimmered green like emeralds in the July sun. They sported two bulbous, purple orbs for what looked like eyes, and a pair of thin antennae waggled atop their heads. They reminded many people watching of large walking stick insects. Murmurs in the crowd agreed: the visitors were hideous or scary or monstrous or a combination of the three.

The tallest creature raised its long arms high into the air and a reverent silence broke over the buzzing spectators. Collectively, the crowd held their breath in anticipation. The visitor gazed across the gathered throngs, spindly appendages still held high, looking not unlike an alien Moses about to part the Red Sea.

"Salutations," it said, its voice scratchy and high-pitched like an untuned violin. "Those of Earth, we have but one thing to say."

Not a whisper could be heard as the multitudes stood in silent awe. History was unfolding before their eyes.

"Our navigational charts need updating," the thing screeched, "does anyone know the quickest way to the Gamora Nebula?"

SAFARI

Crenshaw's long grey fingers deftly tapped at the glowing navigation panel in front of him. He pulled back on the throttle and brought his ship to a high-hover position. "This is ridiculous," he muttered under his breath. "We've been flying in circles *all* day. This is the last time we taxi a couple of wannabe filmmakers to earth; give me good ol' tourists any day."

His co-pilot, Nigel, leaned in close to Crenshaw and pointed a three-fingered hand behind his shoulder, "If these two *yahoos* would take my advice and search a trailer park or a mall—"

One of the passengers, sitting behind them, lurched forward and stuck his bulbous head between the two pilots. "Look, I already told you guys," he said, "We want footage of them in the *wild*. It's too easy to find them in a colony, and Gordy and I will never win an award shooting *easy,* you know. We need them in the natural, we need them—"

"Alright already *Morris*," Crenshaw snapped. He

shooed Morris back with his hand. "We'll scan this lake to our left. Okay? Now, you and your buddy, *please* stay seated and be quiet."

Crenshaw gave his co-pilot a knowing glance and tilted the throttle, veering the ship towards the lake. Morris plopped dejectedly back into his seat and fiddled with the holo-cam in his lap. His assistant, Gordy, rummaged through their travel bags.

The ship silently glided over the shimmering blue surface of the lake and the four travelers scanned the optical view monitor searching for a subject. A small object bobbing on the water appeared on the horizon.

"There!" Morris jumped up again and pointed excitedly at the screen, "There's one in the water vessel."

An annoyed Nigel swiveled his seat to face Morris, "It's called a 'fishing boat'—Geez. If you're going to make a documentary, you might want to learn about your subjects *first*." He turned back to Crenshaw shaking his head in disapproval.

As the passengers leaned forward to scrutinize the screen, Crenshaw adjusted a dial and lowered their altitude. He gently edged the craft closer for a better view, stopping just twenty meters from a small boat.

Sitting in the boat was a Man. He was wearing strange green rubbery pants and holding a pole of sorts with a string dangling from it to the water. With a shocked expression for a human face, he eyed their floating airship as they slowly approached him. A floppy hat pierced with a dozen colorful hooks capped his cranium, and a thin wisp of smoke curled upwards from a little burning white stick stuck in his lips. He sat completely still; his mouth gaped open, and his unblinking eyes fixed on their silvery craft.

"Yes," Morris said in a hushed whisper, "He's perfect."

The four sat in silence, crowded around the screen, watching the Man in the boat staring back at them. The Man didn't move.

"Alright now," Crenshaw cleared his throat, breaking the tension. "Let's get this over with. We'll beam him up to the loading bay. The transport beam only works for living biological specimens, so you won't be able to film his garments or any of his tools. I still don't feel comfortable doing this but—"

"But," interrupted Morris, "Gordy and I paid you good money to get close-ups, and that's *why* you're doing it." Morris winked at his friend.

Morris and Gordy hurriedly picked through their satchels, grabbing various pieces of equipment, and slinging filming gear over their backs.

"Ready!" called Morris. "Got everything, Gord?"

Gordy nodded excitedly.

Crenshaw returned to the control panel, swiping his finger across the illuminated touchpad. A round red dot appeared on the screen, which he centered on the image of the Man in his boat. He rotated a dial and looked around at the others in the cabin, his finger poised above the blinking button in front of him. "Aaand go!"

The space travelers quickly scuttled out of the cabin, their short legs a flurry as they raced the length of the corridor leading to the loading bay. Crenshaw passed his palm over the touchpad to the side of the entrance. The door slid open with a swish, and the four little pale bodies scampered into the bay.

The naked Man was lying on a small oval bench in the nearly empty room. His eyes were shut, his body limp and motionless.

"Okay," said Crenshaw, "He's stunned, so use the paralyzer-ray now, before he wakes up."

Morris and Gordy looked at each other in embarrassed silence. Gordy hung his head and stared at the floor.

"Uh," Morris fumbled, "Yeah... I think we might've forgot to bring one."

Crenshaw slapped a hand to his large forehead in exasperation. "Are you kidding me?"

"Well with the all the camera gear and the excitement—"

"Amateurs." Nigel clucked.

"Look," Crenshaw pleaded. "He'll be coming around any moment; just keep him *calm*. If I can reactivate the transport beam—"

The four suddenly turned their attention back to the Man lying on the bench. The Man's eyelids fluttered as a groan slipped from his lips. Morris flipped the switch on his camera and aimed it towards the Man. "This is great!" he whispered excitedly.

In an instant, the Man's eyes flashed open and he lurched upright on the table. His jaw dropped as his eyes focused on the four small grey figures huddled across the room.

They watched him.

He stared at them.

No one moved.

"Gordy," Morris hissed. "Talk to him. Get the Intergalactic Translator."

Gordy nodded and pulled a small black S-shaped device from his satchel. He tapped in the code for *Human: English* and the device hummed to life.

Thank you for using the Intergalactic Translator Model

5423-6, the mechanical voice intoned, *Translating... Human... English. Please have both parties speak into their respective side of the unit. Speak now...*

Gordy raised the device to his mouth. His three companions held their breath as he stepped towards the Man. Gordy gulped. The Man's eyes darted between the three figures then shot back to Gordy as he cautiously approached the bench. With a sudden jerk, the Man's leg struck out, kicking the translator out of Gordy's hands and sending it clattering across the floor. Nigel and Crenshaw jumped out of the way as the Translator crashed into the wall behind them. A broken shard of the device skittered to Nigel's feet. Gordy cautiously edged backward, his empty hands splayed open, held up in mid-air. The wide-eyed Man sat transfixed, as if frozen in time, his leg sticking straight out.

"Fantastic," Nigel muttered sarcastically as he stooped to pick up the shard at his feet. "He broke the translator," he held up the little scrap of black metal for the others to see, "and it appears to be *our* side of the microphone."

The translator stammered dully on the floor, *Speak... now... speak... Thank you... Thank you...*

Morris lowered his camera and looked to Crenshaw and Nigel. "Well, now what? Didn't one of you say you can speak the human languages?"

"No we didn't, Morris," Nigel sneered, putting his hands on his hips. "Crenshaw and I can just *understand* some of their words! We can't speak their jabbering tongue."

Morris glanced over to the Man. "Well, how do we deal with him?"

Nigel sighed. "Well, *usually*, you bring a *paralyzer-ray*

for this!"

Crenshaw stroked his chin and stared thoughtfully at the Man still sitting with leg out like a petrified tree limb. "Maybe we should present him with the universal token of goodwill—the Rod-of-Peace?" Unanimously, the others nodded their heads in agreement. "Over there, Gordy," he pointed, "it's behind the crates."

Gordy trotted to the corner of the bay where several crates were neatly stacked one on another. He briefly disappeared behind the cartons and reappeared a moment later wheeling a large black box with rollers at its base. On top of the box rested a polished glass orb, from which, a long thin silver rod jutted out the side. Gordy carefully pushed the Rod-of-Peace towards the Man.

Nigel cleared his throat, lifted his eyes upwards, clasped his hands behind his back, and began to ceremoniously recite the customary salutation, "Greetings fellow Galactic Being. Despite the language barriers, we present to you the Rod-of-Peace as a gesture of goodwill. As the rod extends from the sphere, so does our offering of peace extend to you."

While Nigel was speaking, Gordy pivoted the Rod-of-Peace to face the Man.

The Man, unblinking, watched as Gordy first pointed to the long rod and then to him. The color in his face drained and his eyes bulged out of their sockets. Gordy smiling, tapped on the rod and leveled his finger at the Man.

"Eeeaaah!"

The screaming man leaped from the bench, collided with the Rod-of-Peace, and sent it spinning madly on its rollers. The long metal rod swung round in a wide circle before connecting solidly with the back of Gordy's head sending him sprawling, face first, to the floor.

Eeeahhh... ahhh, the Translator repeated in monotone.

"Stop him! Stop him!" Crenshaw shouted, clasping his hands to his head.

In a frenzy, the Man raced across the bay and launched himself violently against the closed bay door. Furiously pounding the door with one clenched fist, his other hand swatted the air behind his bare buttocks, warding off the imagined attackers.

"Haaaalp!" he shrieked. "Y'all ain't gonna probe me! That's virgin territory! Alien scum, get away from me!"

Virgin... alien... get... me... echoed the broken mechanical voice.

Offended, Nigel looked to Crenshaw and piously held his hand over his heart. "I should think not," he sniffed, *"I'm married."*

The frantic Man bellowed as he alternated between smashing the door with his fists and protecting his rear flank with waving hands. Crenshaw motioned to Nigel, and yelled above the din, "C'mon let's both tackle a leg and drag him back to the transport beam!" Nigel bobbed his head in the affirmative and started towards the raging Man. A grinning Morris jumped to the top of a crate for a better vantage point; his camera still recording footage of the excitement. Gordy remained face down, comatose on the floor.

As the Man's hands clawed at the bay exit, his knuckles brushed the touchpad. With a fluid movement, the door quickly slid open and the Man tumbled into the corridor. At that same moment, Nigel, racing towards the Man, tripped over the still-sputtering translator and slammed into the Rod-of-Peace, sending both items crashing into the hallway and shattering the glass orb that held the rod into shiny debris. Amidst the tumult, Gordy staggered to his feet, rubbing the lump on the back of his head, while Morris, shivering with glee, kept filming the unfolding debacle.

Crenshaw, seeing his moment of opportunity vanish, let out a cry, and flung himself at the Man's legs, grasping the Man's bare ankles with his hands.

The Man, panting and with a crazed look in his eyes, bolted down the length of hallway leading towards the pilot's cabin, Crenshaw's small grey figure still holding tight and flopping behind him.

"Haaalp!" shrieked the Man.

"Haaalp!" pleaded Crenshaw.

Haaalp echoed the translator.

Nigel scrambled over the remains of the Rod-of-Peace and grabbed its long silver shaft. "Hang on, Crenshaw, don't let him go!" he cried. He galloped after Crenshaw and the Man, waving the rod above his head and yelling, "Stop him, stop him!"

"Wait for me! This is award-winning stuff!" Morris cried, running after the raucous procession, his holo-cam held high.

Gordy, still dazed, staggered down the hall, bringing up the rear of the parade.

The Man lunged into the open cockpit still dragging a flailing Crenshaw behind him. In a frenzy of what must have been desperation, the Man whirled about the cabin, flipping toggle switches, jabbing buttons, and banging on monitor screens. The ship violently lurched forward as he spun a row of knobs.

Crenshaw, in a bleak attempt to guard the navigation panels, slapped the Man's hands with a flurry of swats. "Stopitstopitstopitstopit," he chanted.

The Man grabbed Crenshaw's spindly grey arm, yanked it to his mouth, and bit down like an animal.

"Yaaahhh," screeched a horrified Crenshaw, "He's eating me!"

Nigel reached the cabin and catapulted to the seat behind the Man. "Spit him out, you savage!" he commanded. Wielding the Rod-of-Peace in clenched hand, he drew back and rained down a furious torrent of whacks upon the Man's noggin. "Take that!" he cried heroically.

A giddy Morris followed close behind, but jumped to the side, pressing his back to the wall to stay clear of the fierce attack, the goodwill token now a punishing silver blur in the hand of Nigel. "Keep it up, this is great stuff," Morris shouted to no one in particular and zoomed in his holo-cam for a close-up of the action.

The Man dropped Crenshaw and spun an outstretched arm around and behind him to stop the barrage. The blow knocked the Rod-of-Peace out of Nigel's hand and sent it sailing through the air and into the forehead of Gordy who had just managed to stumble through the doorway. For the second time that day, Gordy crumpled to the floor.

After a quick inspection of his mauled arm, Crenshaw crawled underneath the front navigation panel for safety. He shot a glance to Nigel, who had jumped onto the back of the crazed Man. The Man was now spinning in wild circles attempting to fling him off. Crenshaw craned his neck to find Morris, who was pressed to the corner, recording his video with trembling exhilaration. "Morris, activate the emergency escape portal!" barked Crenshaw. Morris pulled the camera away from his eye and pondered the idea for a moment. "Do it *now!*" commanded Crenshaw.

Morris, looking not a little disappointed, slammed his hand down on a large, bright red button on a panel behind him. Instantly, a wide floor-to-ceiling portal flashed open on the wall of the cabin. Bright sunlight streamed in, and the cool lake breeze filled the cockpit with a whoosh.

The desperate Man whipped his head to see the newly appeared exit and rushed to the portal and its promise of freedom. "Ah-ha!" he exclaimed. When he got to the side and looked over the edge to the turquoise water twenty meters below him, he instinctively grasped the sides of the door and wrenched himself backward, away from the opening.

"Oh no, you don't!" Crenshaw yelled at the Man. He called to Nigel and Morris, "All three of us, get him—now!"

Crenshaw, Nigel, and Morris rushed to the back of the Man, as he still gripped the sides of the portal with a white-knuckled intensity. With a collective grunt, three skinny grey legs simultaneously shoved the bawling Man out of the exit, where he tumbled head over feet to the lake beneath them. Morris, camera in hand, peered over the edge, following the spectacle to its conclusion which culminated in a substantial splash of water.

The three figures stood at the doorway panting and staring at the scene below. Gordy, rubbing the front of his head, shuffled behind them and followed their gaze. The sputtering Man had managed to swim back to his boat and was crawling over its wooden side.

"Phew," sighed a grinning Morris after a moment or two of silence, "Well, the good news is, I recorded it all."

Without a word, Crenshaw and Nigel exchanged a tired glance. Crenshaw reached out, grabbed the camera out of Morris's hand, and flung it as far as he could. The golden sunlight glinted off the shiny holo-cam as it flipped and twirled to the lake below. Nigel picked up the silver Rod-of-Peace at his feet and swung a hard whack to the back of Morris's head.

A moment later, the portal slid shut and the four travelers were soaring higher into the sky. They could still make out the Man far below them, shaking a clenched fist raised in the air.

PATENT PENDING

"Trust me," the little gray dude said, "go ahead and jump."

I cocked my eyebrow. "I seem to remember dying the last time I trusted you."

The hairless, half-pint folded his long arms and scowled. "And didn't I bring you right back to life? Didn't I? You always manage to forget about that. Now, *trust me*... jump."

I took a slow breath and licked my lips. My mouth was dry. "Is it going to hurt as much as the last time?"

"Errr... no," he said, narrowing his black, almond-shaped eyes. "At least... I don't think so." His slit of a mouth curled upwards in his best impression of a human smile.

I stared at the shimmering blue portal swirling in front of me, its plasma energy crackling with intensity. The statically charged hairs on the back of my neck stood on end.

The last time I jumped through the portal it felt like diving into a pool of broken glass. Of course, the pain had only lasted a moment before I dropped dead. The little gray dude had floated me to his medi-pod and brought me back to life, a fact he won't let me forget. He later admitted that he had 'miscalculated' the portal's settings. Unfortunately, even the best technology is only as good as its operator, and I seem to have the alien version of a circus clown running the show.

"Well?" he prodded. "Do you want to go home or not?"

"Of course I do," I said. "I'm just not eager to have my brain fried again, alright? For the record, it wasn't my idea to abduct me and keep me prisoner for... How long have I been up here anyway? Two weeks?"

The little gray bugged out his eyes and extended the length of his neck. (He does that whenever he's irritated, and it always reminds me of a giraffe.) "I'm hurt. I'm really hurt that you say this, Human Dave. Have I not shown you the wonders of space and science? Have I not taken good care of you during this time? You've not been a prisoner, you've been my guest."

For an alien, he speaks great English, but, man, the drama.

"Look, shorty, I've only been your 'guest,' because you needed a guinea pig, and now you can't configure your experimental portal transporter-thingy to get me back, you moron."

He balled his fists and jumped to the top of the blinking control panel. "I'm a short moron, am I?" He waved his little fists in the air, ready for a duel.

I closed my eyes and counted to ten. We were already on each other's nerves, and I probably shouldn't be offending him. After all, he was a hothead, and I didn't want to start an interplanetary war.

I opened my eyes and mashed my fingertips together. "I appreciate this... *experience*," I replied in a controlled tone. "I really do. I suppose you could have kidnapped me, probed my who-knows-what, and left me for dead somewhere if you had wanted to."

My little 'host' grimaced and hopped off the control panel. His small frame landed with a soft thunk on the metallic floor.

I continued, "And I *have* seen some cool stuff. I mean, how many humans can say they've seen Saturn's rings close-up? But— and this is a big 'but' here— by this time, I'm sure my parents think I'm either a corpse or a runaway, and my girlfriend is probably back with her football stud ex-boyfriend. I'm just a little worried about all the time that has elapsed since... 'being your guest.'" I spread a wide plastic smile on my face.

I could tell by the way my captor nodded and yowled he was amused. When this little gray guy laughs, it almost sounds like an alley cat in heat.

"Oh, you funny Human Dave," he giggled. "Is that what you're worried about?" He yowled some more and stomped his feet. After his fits of delighted screeching subsided, he sighed. "I already thought of that after our last attempt. This is the beauty of my invention: I've attached a time-dilation module to the quantum displacement drive." He threw his arms open as if revealing a grand surprise. "You see? I'm going to transport you back to the same moment we left Earth. You have nothing to fear."

I glanced out the ship's viewport into the star-cluttered, inky blackness of space. "Well, the other issue is the fact that we appear to be hundreds of miles outside of Earth's atmosphere. You're sure this thing will transport me all the way back home, right? I don't want to end up in Antarctica or worse, like on the moon or something."

The little gray dude drummed his thin pallid fingers on his bulbous noggin. "Human Dave, *trust me*."

"Yeah, well..." I couldn't think of any more excuses to delay the inevitable.

"Don't worry," he threw up his hands for emphasis, "I'll beam you right back to thirty-two Cole Street in Kansas City, United States. Okay?"

I sighed and turned my attention back to the whirling portal. I shook my head and muttered a comment about "crispy brains."

He rubbed his hands together and added, "And if it works, I'm going to make a lot of money back on my planet. To think of it: collecting specimens from outside the atmosphere. Ha!" He gave me an awkward thumbs-up. "Thanks for helping with this project, Human Dave."

You didn't give me a choice, moron, I thought.

"I knew that selecting an adolescent specimen for experimentation was the best choice," he said with a wink. "Less chance of permanent neuronal damage, you know."

I rolled my eyes. "In other words, there's a good chance I might come out of this a drooling cretin?"

He shrugged, "Eh, probably not?" He pointed his finger towards the portal. "Now, if you would..."

Wiping my sweaty palms on my jeans, I took a deep breath. My heart thumped in my chest and I gulped, swallowing my fear. "Okay, well, here goes nothing." I squeezed my eyes shut and jumped.

Pain.

A shrill whine screamed in my ears threatening to tear my head apart, and a dizzying swirl of colors and light danced in front of my eyes like a psychedelic whirlpool. Gradually, I came to the realization I was on my hands and knees, my head hanging low. I slowed down my heaving breaths as my senses returned. The odors of dirt and earthy manure filled my nostrils. I inhaled them deeply.

Earth. Home.

No drool, that's a good sign. Wait—manure?

I blinked my eyes and squinted in the brilliant sunlight. With trembling, unsteady limbs, I carefully rose to my feet and patted dust off my knees. This wasn't my street, was it?

My eyes focused and I gazed across an unfamiliar dirt road. I saw a rickety wooden building and a hand-painted sign hanging above it: Kansas City's Famous Cole Street Saloon.

A dirty faced man in a wide-brimmed hat and spurred boots sauntered through a set of creaky swinging doors at the building's entrance. He spat a gob of brown juice into a spittoon at his feet, then glared in my direction.

As horses trotted past and curious onlookers gathered to gawk and point, I realized the little gray dude had sent me back to my home on Cole Street as promised. Of course, he was a couple of hundred years off.

Moron, I thought.

THE COUNTDOWN OF A LIFETIME

Jerome knew he had thirty-two years and nineteen days left to live. He was pleased with the fact. That number gave him a total of sixty-nine years and forty days, which is a fine length of life by anyone's standards, *especially* nowadays.

Jerome straightened his bow-tie, adjusted his round spectacles, and glanced at the clock on the wall. *Only five minutes to go*, he chuckled to himself. Above the clock hung a small plaque that read: Population Protectorate Office #259. He opened his desk drawer to make sure the paperclips, calculator, file tabs, hair comb, and three black pens were all in a neat arrangement. A blinking light on his view-monitor caught his eye and he quickly turned his attention to the screen. Poking a finger at the switch on the side of his headset he cleared his throat.

"Protectorate office two-five-nine, this is Jerome speaking. How may I be of assistance today?" A woman's shrill voice prattled on the other end of the line. Jerome briefly adjusted the volume setting.

"Why, good afternoon Mrs. Wallace. Fine day we're having. Hmmm? You say your husband began beeping? Oh my, I'm terribly sorry to hear that. Well, as you know, after the beeping begins, he has twenty-four to seventy-two hours left to get his affairs in order. I'm sure that now would be an excellent time to say 'goodbyes' and what-have-you. Perhaps one last romantic dinner for the both of you tonight?" The woman on the line was hysterically sobbing, and Jerome pressed his index finger to his lips while trying to understand her.

"What's that? You believe there's an error?" he asked, shocked. "Mrs. Wallace," he soothed in a soft conciliatory tone, "Mistakes are few and far between, I assure you. No, no. I don't have access to his Expiration Date. Only the Directors of the Population Protectorate have that information. However, if you believe his Timer is malfunctioning our service technicians would be more than happy to scan it for errors. Shall I schedule you for an appointment? Fine, fine." Jerome's fingers clacked away on the keypad in front of his view-monitor.

"Let's see," he said, "How does next Monday at 1:00 pm sound?" More muffled sobbing came from the woman on the line and Jerome turned down the volume control on his earpiece a second time. "Really now, Mrs. Wallace, there's no need for hysterics. Next Monday is the best I can do. After all, this is Friday and our technicians don't work the weekends. Now, I thought you would be grateful, Mrs. Wallace. The technicians are very busy and it wouldn't be fair to other Citizens who already *have* appointments. I'm sure you understand. Yes, yes— Of *course,* we'll let you know if anything opens up sooner. Let's just hope for the best with the timing of things, shall we? Thank you for calling, Mrs. Wallace, have a wonderful evening and remember, The Population Protectorate is here to *save you*."

Jerome removed his headset and laid it carefully on the desk. He opened the drawer and brought out his small fine-toothed comb. With tidy strokes, he smoothed the few remaining hairs on his shiny scalp into order. He placed the comb back into the appropriate compartment and slid the drawer shut. With one finger, Jerome gently scratched around the dime-sized black button at the base of his skull. His Timer never irritated him, but it could be... *itchy* at times. He sighed happily, hit the power switch on his computer, picked up his brown leather briefcase, and slid on his grey overcoat. *Fine day, fine day*, he thought to himself as he hummed a little ditty and walked out of his cubicle and down the hallway.

***

"Jerome," Mr. Gould called out, "Would you step into my office for a moment?" Jerome hurried into the Management office and nodded his head at the Director. He recalled the first time he met Director Gould in this same office several years ago. Jerome's personnel file had been on the desk splayed open when he had stolen a glance at his own Expiration Date.

"Good evening, Director Gould. Pleasure to see you," Jerome chirped. "I was just on my way home."

"You, m'boy," and here Mr. Gould jabbed his finger in the air towards Jerome, "are doing some mighty fine work."

Jerome beamed. "Why, *thank you,* sir! Always a pleasure, I'm sure."

The Director lowered his fat chin and peered over his glasses. "Don't think it's not being noticed Jerome," Mr. Gould said. "I've been asked to name an Assistant Managerial Assistant recently and your name came up."

Jerome's pudgy jowls rolled upwards and broke into a grin. "Oh, why, thank you, sir," he exclaimed. "Marvelous news, sir!"

"Yes, yes," Director Gould replied and clenched his bushy eyebrows together. "We do important work here and we need the kind of man who can run, er, *help* run things like a tight ship."

"Yes, of course," Jerome said, still smiling.

"The Timer is far too useful and important a tool, for the well-being of our Citizens. We don't need some nincompoop, who can't keep their numbers straight, in charge of things. I assure you, m'boy," and here Mr. Gould pointed upwards and ceremoniously wagged his finger, "if you keep up the good work, you will climb to *new heights* on the ladder of success."

Jerome could not hide his thrill and shook the Director's hand with gusto. "Thank you, sir, *thank you*!"

Mr. Gould waved him off and Jerome hurried out of the office with a bounce in his step. As he was leaving, Frank Wills walked by and Jerome heard Mr. Gould call out, "Frank! Step into my office for a moment." Frank disappeared into the office behind him. Jerome happily continued down the hallway as Mr. Gould's voice trailed off, "You, m'boy, are doing some mighty fine work..."

Yes sir, Jerome thought merrily to himself as he

polished his spectacles with a white handkerchief, *A-M-A. Won't that be nice? I'm sure a little plaque with gold-lettering: Assistant Managerial Assistant, would be in order. Yes sir, quite nice.*

As he waited for the elevator, he glanced at a poster plastered on the side wall. It was a happy picture of a smiling couple holding their newborn infant. Above the child, a grinning Doctor was implanting a Timer into the baby's head. The poster had a painted picture of the Timer; a little black button with two electrodes jutting out. The poster exclaimed: *The electrodes are painlessly placed around the brain-stem for efficient action!* The blocky neon-yellow text at the bottom read: *Save the planet Ma and Pa! Either sterilize or time your Baby, it's the LAW!*

The elevator doors slid open and Jerome pressed the button for the sky-walk. He recalled his first days of training at the Population Protectorate. He remembered learning everything there was to know about the Timer. The Government, in its wisdom, *knew* that population growth was surpassing the available resources needed for life. Famine, water shortages, epidemics – all of these problems were solved. And to think, all it took was a tiny, little, black button. Jerome absent-mindedly scratched the back of his head and stepped onto the sky-walk.

***

The tram in the sky-walk tunnel whistled as it sped towards the outskirts of the city. A man jostled through the work-wearied crowd of commuters and tugged at Jerome's arm.

"Jerome? How ya doing?"

Jerome turned around and smiled, "Why Bill, good to see you."

"How're things in Citizen Time Service?" Bill asked.

"Can't complain, can't complain." Jerome brushed off his sleeves and sniffed. "Fact is, I've been mentioned for AMA." He beamed.

"No. You don't say?" Bill said with surprise. "Well, congratulations. I've got a little bit of news myself. I've been told I'm next in line for Associate Technician Assistant."

"Well now isn't that splendid?" Jerome replied, shaking Bill's hand. "Well done, well done."

Bill tugged his trousers up and shoved his hands into his pockets. "Yep, I was a member of a team who helped the technicians, who helped the programmers, who helped the Directors come up with the new Fair-Time-Algorithm. Yes, sir. We've made the Timer even more fair now. The Timer's new algorithm ensures that everybody, and I mean *everybody*, has an average, yet fair, lifetime. I'm quite proud of it. Naturally, we have to have the occasional expedient Countdowns in order to keep things truly *average*."

"Naturally," said Jerome thoughtfully. He paused, then pointed at the bottom of the plasti-glass tram. "Look at this city, Bill." He shook his finger. "It's people like you and me that ensure there's room enough for everyone down there." Jerome stuck out his bottom lip and went on, "Oh sure, I know the Timer's not perfect. Maybe there's a mistake *once in a great while*. Maybe a person, here or there, gets a little *less* time for one reason or another." Jerome shrugged his shoulders and raised his hands. "But overall, who can complain?"

There was a bit of commotion in the tram compartment as a man pushed his way through the packed car and found an empty seat near where Jerome was standing. A dull beeping noise was coming from the man's neck. He dropped into the seat and stared ahead with a blank expression; his eyes glazed and bloodshot. Despite the crowd, the other passengers gave him a wide berth as if the air around the man was poisoned. He said nothing, but every so often would pull a damp handkerchief from a breast pocket and dab his brow. The commuters near him stared hard into their newspapers or out the windows. Two women standing near the man clucked disapprovingly.

"Really," said one woman, "I should think it's not appropriate to be on the tram in *his* condition."

"I agree," replied the other nodding her head, "How very rude. You would think he has *better* things to do."

The man briefly glanced at the women and then looked in Jerome's direction. Jerome pretended not to notice and nervously smoothed his bow tie. He silently agreed with the two ladies, *It's very inconsiderate of the fellow to make others feel uncomfortable at this time.* Jerome thought, *I hope he has the decency to finish somewhere a little more private.* Jerome detested the hubbub following a public Expiration; the awkward flurry of activity as the Disposal Technicians appeared on location and scrambled about the *Expired,* wrapping them up in green bags to ship to the Processing and Disposal Center. It was a most embarrassing scene and he tried to avoid it whenever he could.

The tram whined as it came to its final stop. Jerome felt a rush of relief as he buttoned his coat and picked up his briefcase. He turned back towards Bill. "Congratulations again Bill, and good job."

"The same to you!" Bill called out as he too made his way through the crowd.

Jerome watched as streams of passengers flowed around the beeping man while he slowly shuffled to the exit. Jerome joined the hurried flow and stepped out of the tram and into the brisk evening air.

His humming turned to a cheerful whistle as he walked home.

***

Mr. Gould had just slipped on his overcoat when the phone rang. He glanced at the clock and yawned. He customarily worked late and tonight was no exception. Plopping back into his chair, he grabbed the receiver.

"Director Gould speaking," he answered brusquely. "Why Jerome," he lightened his tone, "What can I do for you, m'boy?" He checked the clock again. "Oh, I see, " he said, raising his bushy eyebrows. "Well, that is a shame. Why don't you give Citizen Time Service a call? You of all people should know that. Hmm? Can't get through? Well, what did you expect Jerome? It's Friday evening, very few staff on the weekend shift, you know." Mr. Gould shifted in his chair and looked at the clock for the third time. The voice on the other line frantically chattered on.

"Now, Jerome," Mr. Gould interrupted." "No need to work yourself into a tizzy about this. Mistakes are rare you know, and it's late, and I have a dinner reservation with the Missus. We mustn't keep her waiting now." He let out a sigh of exasperation. "Oh very well, Jerome, hold on while I check." Mr. Gould placed the receiver down and wheeled his chair to the filing cabinet. He thumbed through several folders before pulling Jerome's personnel file. He held his eyeglasses above his nose while reading the cover sheet and picked up the receiver.

"Well now, this *is* embarrassing, " Mr. Gould chuckled, "It seems you're absolutely right, Jerome. Probably some computer glitch somewhere." He smiled. "Just goes to show you, computers can never replace a good man. That's why I admire you, m'boy, you've got a head for numbers. Keep up the good work and you'll go far. Now, I tell you what, come see me in my office *first thing* Monday morning and we'll iron this whole mess out. Good night, Jerome." Mr. Gould hung up the phone and plucked his hat from the back of his office door. He hummed as he strolled down the hall to meet his wife for dinner. *Fine day, fine day*, he thought to himself.

Thank you for purchasing this book. If you've enjoyed these stories, please leave a review on Amazon.

Sign up for our mailing list and be entered to win a FREE autographed copy of any of J.J. Harlan's books. New winner selected every month!

Sign up here:

https://mailchi.mp/f934c2e6967c/jjharlan

ABOUT THE AUTHOR

J.J. Harlan is a science fiction writer located in the magical, mystical land of the Pacific Northwest. When he's not drinking coffee and dreaming up strange worlds, he's hiking in the mountains with his wife, ever on the lookout for a UFO or a friendly bigfoot.

Printed in Great Britain
by Amazon